DM: For my horribly good husband and kids

BL: For Nicholas, my great muse and constant valentine

Sky Pony Press books may be purchased in bulk at special discounts for sales promotion, corporate gifts, fund-raising, or educational purposes. Special editions can also be created to specifications. For details, contact the Special Sales Department, Sky Pony Press, 307 West 36th Street, 11th Floor, New York, NY 10018 or info@skyhorsepublishing.com.

Sky Pony® is a registered trademark of Skyhorse Publishing, Inc.®, a Delaware corporation.

Visit our website at www.skyponypress.com.

10 9 8 7 6 5

Manufactured in China, February 2020
This product conforms to CPSIA 2008

Library of Congress Cataloging-in-Publication Data

Names: Murray, Diana, author. | Langley, Bats, illustrator.
Title: Groggle's monster Valentine / written by Dianna Murray ; illustrated by Bats Langley.
Description: New York, NY : Skyhorse Publishing, [2017] | Summary: Groggle is determined to make the perfect Valentine's Day card for his best friend Snarlina, but there is just one problem--he keeps eating everything he makes.
Identifiers: LCCN 2016050220 (print) | LCCN 2017022023 (ebook) | ISBN 9781510705098 | ISBN 9781510705081 (alk. paper) | ISBN 9781510705098 (ebook)
Subjects: | CYAC: Valentine's Day--Fiction. | Monsters--Fiction. | Best friends--Fiction. | Friendship--Fiction.
Classification: LCC PZ7.1.M876 (ebook) | LCC PZ7.1.M876 Gr 2017 (print) | DDC [E]--dc23
LC record available at https://lccn.loc.gov/2016050220

Cover design by Bats Langley
Cover illustration credit: Bats Langley

Groggle's Monster Valentine

WRITTEN BY
DIANA MURRAY

ILLUSTRATED BY
BATS LANGLEY

SKY PONY PRESS

Sky Pony Press
New York

It was Valentine's night in the dark forest, and Groggle
was still working on his card. It had to be perfect because
it was for Snarlina—his beast friend in the whole wide world.

He found just the right heart-shaped leaves.

Then he gathered up some bog slime and squirted in bold, gooey letters:

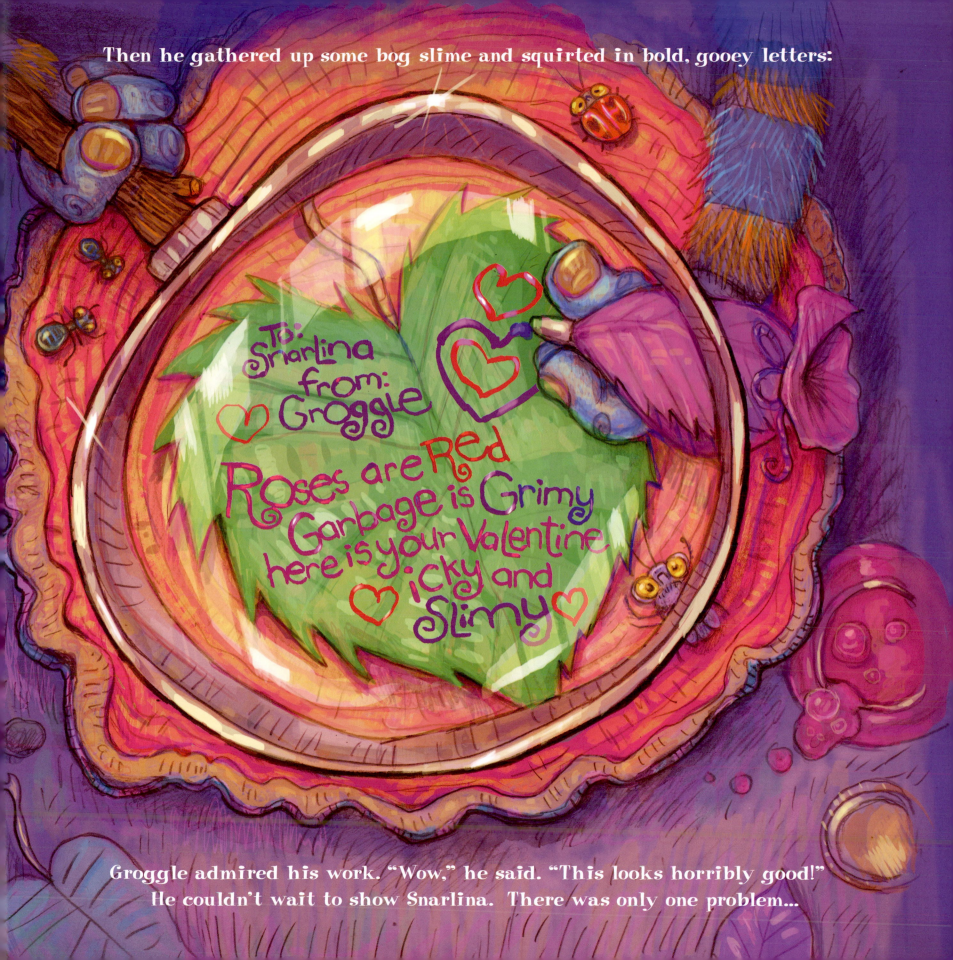

To: Snarlina from: Groggle

Roses are Red
Garbage is Grimy
here is your Valentine
icky and Slimy

Groggle admired his work. "Wow," he said. "This looks horribly good!"
He couldn't wait to show Snarlina. There was only one problem...

He had a monster appetite.

Groggle tried again:

"Grrraaaarrrrrr!"
he growled. "I will NOT eat
another Valentine!"

To make sure he was not hungry,
Groggle whipped up his
favorite snack: ants on a log.

He munched...

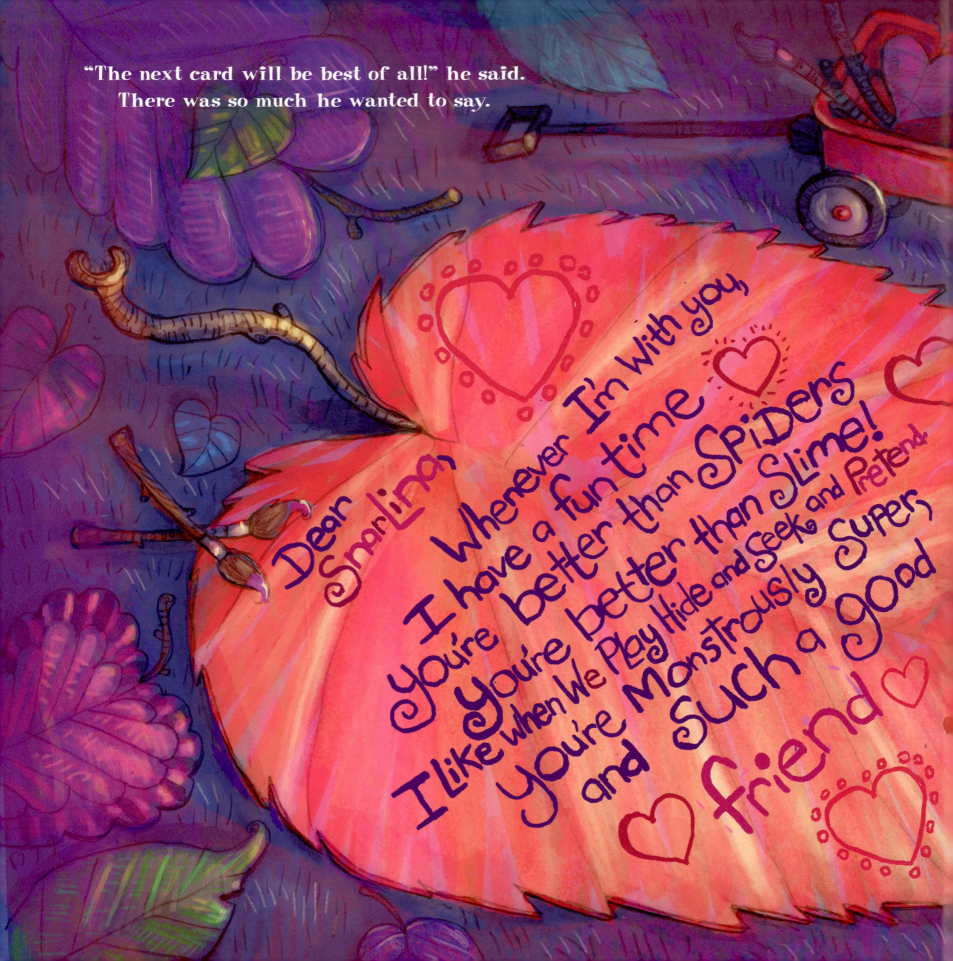

"The next card will be best of all!" he said.
There was so much he wanted to say.

Dear SnarLina,
Whenever I'm with you,
I have a fun time
you're better than SpiDers
you're better than SLime!
I Like when We Play Hide and Seek and Pretend,
You're Monstrously Super,
and Such a good
friend

Then he made a few extras, just in case.

Stomps Loudly
Never Neat
Awfully Fun
Roars a Lot
Likes Lurking
Ill-tempered
Nasty
Always Amazingly
MOnstrous

Dear Snarlina,
Your hair is so tangled.
Your teeth are so Green.
You're the Prettiest Monster that I've Ever Seen.
I LOve how you STOMP
I LOVE how you DrOoL
You're a horribly, horriDly fabuLous Ghoul!
LOVE,
Groggle

Here's a Creepy Valentine. Hope you like the thorny *Vine*. Fangs for being Mine!

Groggle decorated each card with care. He sprinkled them with shiny beetle glitter and tied on snake bows. They looked really, awfully good!

Groggle licked his lips.

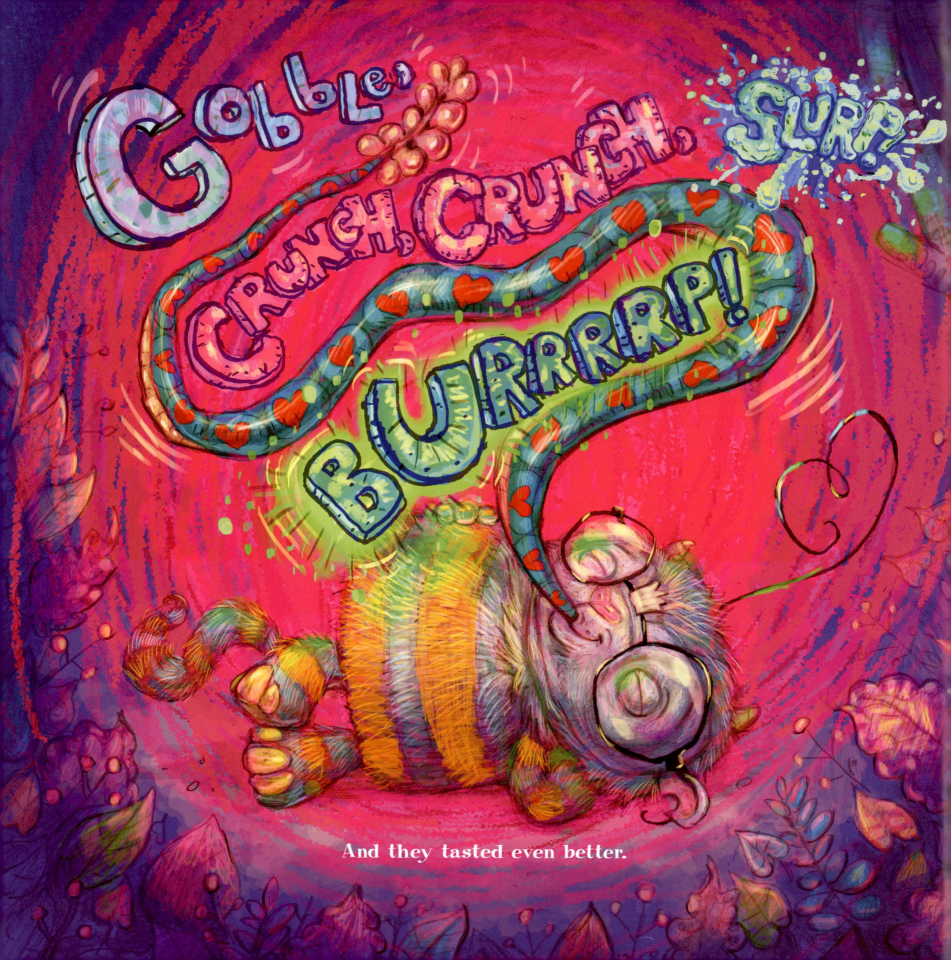

And they tasted even better.

He would go to Snarlina's house with what was left.

Groggle sighed. At least he saved one last bite.

Snarlina flung the door open and growled. Groggle groaned
a little and handed over the half eaten, wrinkled, slobbery card.
There was only one smudgy word left for her to read: FRIEND.

"How terribly sweet," she said with a toothy grin.

Then she gave Groggle a monster hug!

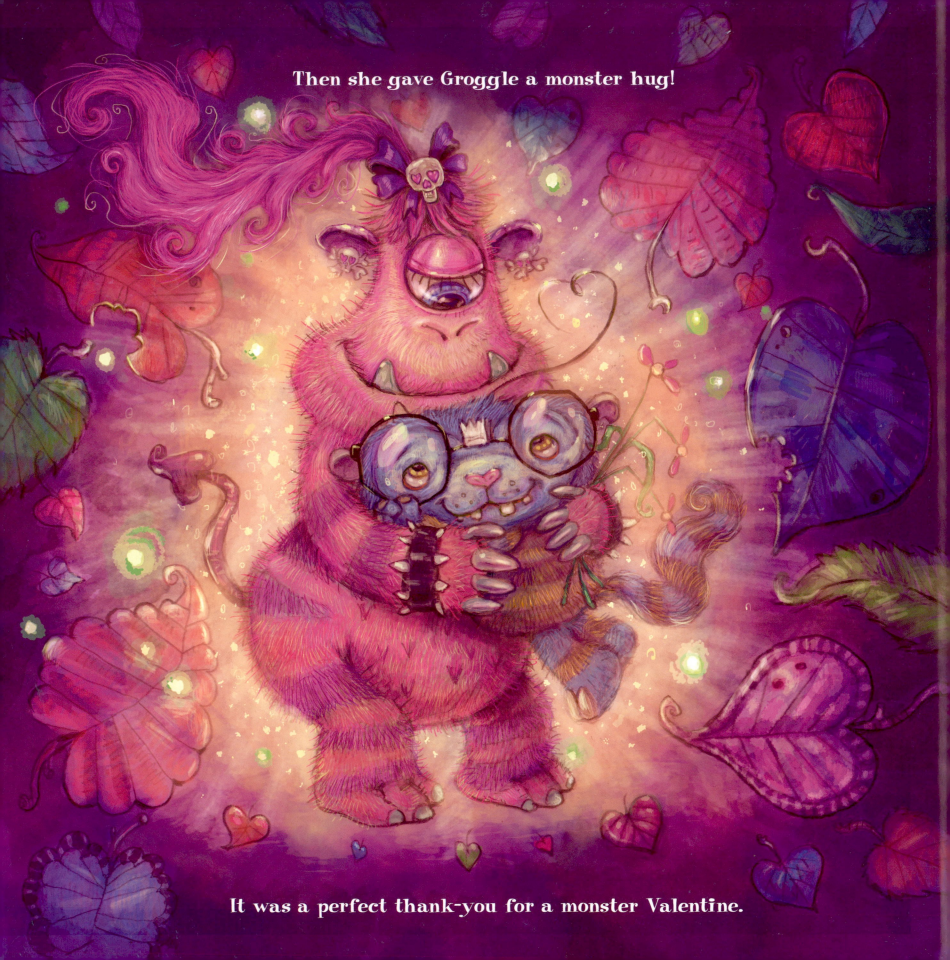

It was a perfect thank-you for a monster Valentine.